The Haunting of Lakeside Woods

Nicole Simon

Published by Nicole Simon, 2024.

This is a work of fiction. Similarities to real people, places, or events are entirely coincidental.

THE HAUNTING OF LAKESIDE WOODS

First edition. February 1, 2024.

Copyright © 2024 Nicole Simon.

ISBN: 979-8224652129

Written by Nicole Simon.

The Haunting of Lakeside Woods

Nicole Simon

© Copyright 2023 - All rights reserved.

Chapter 10: Josh
Chapter 11: The Fight
Chapter 12: The Bodies
Chapter 13: Ending

Chapter 1: The Woods

It was the high, keening sound that woke her up. Sarah turned over, still half-asleep, and tried to cover her ears. It only got louder, and now fully awake, she sat up in bed. There were dark shadows in the corners of the room, and for a moment she forgot where she was. She felt the old, familiar panic creeping back, squeezing her throat like Josh used to during his rage episodes. In her half-asleep state, she almost thought he was still in bed next to her. She reached out with her hand, and fell back, satisfied when she found that the bed next to her was empty.

Buddy barked from beside the bed, and she was now wide awake. When she remembered where she was, her panic faded. She had moved into the cabin on the edge of the woods earlier that day, and that was why there were boxes stacked all over the bedroom. It was the boxes that had created the dark shadows at the foot of her bed. She had been too tired to unpack everything and had just left them there, intending to get to work the next day. The move was far away from her former home, so her furniture and other belongings had only arrived at the cabin in the late afternoon.

Buddy, her Labrador, had been well-behaved during the long drive out here; he had slept most of the way and only barked once when he had to urinate. She had ended up eating her lunch in a picnic spot while she waited for Buddy to run around and finish his business.

Sarah had left her former home in the early hours of the previous morning after Josh had left for work. He didn't know that she had been planning on leaving him for a while. They had been to therapy a couple of times, but the only conclusion she had come to was that she needed to get away from him. The therapist supported her decision when she saw her alone.

Planning her escape and buying the house had taken several months, and she had only been able to do it because of the encouragement and support she had received from the therapist. Ms. Laing had told her Josh would never change, and that she had to get away to save her sanity and her own life. Her escape was only possible because her previous two books had sold well, and Josh didn't know she had hidden a substantial amount of money in a secret bank account. He always complained about having to pay his own way, since she was a well-known writer, and she should be rolling in the cash. He always maintained that if she wasn't making money, she was doing something wrong. Josh once even suggested that maybe her books were too intellectual, and people found them boring. He said she needed to write more violent books with a lot of sex in them. That was Josh. Lately, she didn't know what she had ever seen in him in the first place. He had been handsome, and she had low self-esteem. She had just been grateful that a good-looking man would be interested in her. However, she soon found out that they had nothing much in common, and he wasn't interested in what she had to say in real life, or in her books.

When they'd first started therapy, she kept hoping that things would improve between her and Josh, but it turned out that Ms. Laing was right. The bruises were still on her body from where Josh had beaten her two days ago because she had said something innocent that offended him in some way. Buddy had saved her. Josh usually locked Buddy outside when he was home, but this time the dog had been in the kitchen, eating his breakfast. He must have heard the screaming and shouting, because he ran to her aid, growling, and launched himself at Josh, knocking him over onto the floor. Josh, who was scared of dogs, had gone hysterical and tried to fend off the angry dog by smacking him. Fortunately for him, the dog had only torn his shirt to pieces.

After Sarah managed to pull Buddy off Josh, he threatened he would have the dog put down, since it had attacked him. He was convinced that the dog would still rip out his throat. That gave her the motivation she needed to get her escape plan going.

Buddy barked again, and that forced her to focus on her present reality. The sound hadn't come again, so it was likely that it had been part of her dream. Perhaps her overstrained mind had created the sound. The therapist had said she could experience intrusive memories and nightmares. She'd given Sarah a prescription for tranquilizers, but she had never taken them.

Sarah patted the bed.

"Hey, boy. Who's a good boy?"

The Labrador grinned and jumped on the bed next to her, where he placed his big head in her lap. She patted his head and he sighed contentedly.

"Sorry, boy, I'll cook your chicken tomorrow. I know you don't like the pellets."

She had been too tired to cook the dog his chicken after the long day she'd had, and he gave her a disapproving frown when she placed the bowl of pellets in front of him.

She was about to go back to sleep with Buddy next to her when the keening wail came again from the woods. It made her hair stand on end, and she shivered. There was probably some natural explanation, but she had an overactive imagination, and she envisaged all kinds of horrible creatures. Buddy answered the wail with his own deep moan, which turned into a growl. Sarah hugged the dog close to her. Her stomach was in knots, and she was starting to feel like she felt after a fight with Josh: rattled and shaky.

Sarah and Buddy sat huddled together until the wail quieted down once more. Could an injured animal be making that sound? She had worked as a volunteer at the zoo, but she never heard any of the animals make a sound that was close to this one. It distressed her that a dying animal might need her help, but she was also afraid to put herself in danger.

Buddy howled again, and she couldn't make out if it was a sympathy howl or if he was simply afraid. She got up and pulled away the blanket she had placed against the window. She hadn't had the time yet to hang curtains. The woods were ink-black and dark, and for a moment she couldn't breathe. She wasn't used to this next-level creepy darkness, as Josh would call it. Why was she still thinking of Josh? She never wanted to see him again. If he ever found her, he would probably kill her for leaving him. She could just imagine his face, and then his violent reaction, when he realized she was gone. He had a tendency to throw and kick things. They often had broken windows, and once he'd broken their expensive television by throwing a plant at it. She had paid for the TV, and he was even madder at her when she refused to replace it.

She had only told Louise, her literary agent, where she went. Sarah took a deep breath in and out while she peered outside. It was so dark; if she went out there now, she honestly wouldn't be able to see her hand before her face. She could take her flashlight with her, but what if whatever was out there was dangerous? Her pepper spray was probably still in the car, but she wasn't going out there to get it.

The strange sound came again, but this time it was lower, and it sounded far away. Buddy barked and pulled at her pajama sleeve. Sighing, she got out of bed. She supposed she could at least go out in the front of the house and see if she could spot anything from there. She would take her strongest flashlight with her. If anything came out of the woods, she could run back into the house and shut the door behind her. She could sprint fast; she had been a track star at her high school.

She worried about Buddy going too far, but he was an obedient dog. He usually stayed close to her and wasn't the type to run off by himself. Sarah walked through to the living room with Buddy by her side. The house was dark, as there was no electricity, and she hadn't had the time to set up solar panels or anything else. Luckily, she had good night vision. She found the flashlight and walked toward the front door. She unlocked it and stepped swiftly outside, only realizing when her feet touched the wooden deck that she had forgotten to put on shoes or slippers. She wasn't planning on going far from the house, so it shouldn't matter.

Sarah walked up and down the deck, shining her light into the forest. It didn't seem like anything out of the ordinary was going on out there.

Once or twice, her eyes played tricks on her, and she thought she could see movement in the trees. At this time of the night, it could likely also be bats flying around. For a moment, she thought she saw white figures moving around, but then she saw it was mist. The woods would disappear in the mist by the early hours of the morning.

Sarah shuddered as she imagined Josh out there, slowly creeping up to the house with a knife or gun in his hand. If Josh came to kill her, he would probably use a knife. She didn't think he had ever touched a gun in his life, but then she also thought she knew him when they'd moved in together. He was so sugary sweet the first few weeks they were dating, but that person disappeared soon enough and wasn't coming back.

She sighed as she paced the deck, not really paying attention to what was happening around her. She had to stop thinking about Josh. Physically she had gotten away from him, but he was still in her head. She had lost three years of her life to his abusive behavior, and she wanted to move on. The therapist had told her that it would take time.

Suddenly, the sound came again, but it was different this time. She could distinctly hear a woman crying. Buddy howled, and then took off, running into the woods. Sarah screamed his name. This was what she had been afraid of all along, but she didn't think he would actually do it. Buddy didn't know the area, so she didn't know if he would find his way back home.

"Buddy! Bad dog! Come back!"

Buddy ignored her and disappeared into the trees. Sarah swore and started running after him. It was only when she was past the first rows of trees that she remembered she wasn't wearing shoes. She had also left the front door of the house open, making herself the perfect target for any person or animal who wanted to get in.

Sarah was used to walking barefoot, which made it easier just to carry on. She couldn't go back without Buddy and would never forgive herself if something happened to him out here. He had belonged to her late dad and was all she had left of him. She knew Buddy wouldn't be with her forever, but she wasn't quite ready for that day yet. Buddy was also getting older and shouldn't be out here by himself. She had noticed recently that some mornings, he got up with difficulty.

She cupped her hands around her mouth.

"Buddy!"

There was no sight or sound of the dog. Sarah walked deeper into the woods. She noticed with unease that the air among the trees smelled stale, like she was in a house that had been closed up for too long and not outside in the fresh air. It felt as if something had been trapped in the woods for years.

"Buddy! You need to come home!"

Her feet were getting sore. Even for her, the terrain was rough, and her calves were starting to ache. Her heartbeat increased, and she felt that panic was slowly taking over. What if she never found Buddy? She had come out here to start a new, happier life, but now she was already facing disaster. Maybe Josh was right when he said she couldn't do anything right and that her writing success was more luck than anything else. There were way better writers out there, but she had just published at the right time. After reading her bestseller, he'd thrown it back in her face and called it women's nonsense. He said her readers were just as crazy as she was.

Sarah focused on her breathing. *Don't panic, you can do this. Buddy can't be far. Think, where would he go?*

She heard a bark in the distance and started running toward it. Suddenly, she was grabbed from behind and lifted in the air. Sarah screamed. The panic she had been trying to suppress rushed over her at once, like a wave that threatened to pull her into the sea and drown her. Her pajamas tore, and she was released from whoever was holding her. Sarah fell to the ground and tried to roll away from her assailant. She didn't get very far, as she collided with one of the giant trees. When she looked back, she felt simultaneously relieved and silly. Her assailant was a huge tree branch. She got to her feet, feeling discouraged. Her nightgown was in tatters, and there was still no sign of Buddy.

Sarah was still thinking about what to do when a large man with a pot belly came striding through the trees. He was carrying a gas lamp, and he smiled brightly when he saw her. The man looked so friendly that it was impossible to be scared of him, even though he was a massive hulk of a man.

"My dear, are you lost? Does the yellow doggy perhaps belong to you? Friendly fellow, he turned up at our house about 15 minutes ago."

Sarah stumbled to the man, who gripped her arm to steady her.

"Careful, dear. I'm Mr. Johnson. My wife and I live just through the trees over there. I assume you must be the lady who bought the cabin on the edge of the woods. Let's fetch your dog, and then I'll walk you back home. My wife has given him something to eat."

Sarah offered him her hand and introduced herself. He took her arm again to help her down the small hill that separated his house from the woods. The light was on at the house, and the place looked friendly and warm. Sarah heard Buddy barking at the house and immediately felt much better.

As they came closer to Mr. Johnson's house, Sarah could see Buddy standing next to a large, sturdy woman, who she assumed must be Mrs. Johnson.

When they reached the bottom, Buddy barked excitedly, ran up to her and sniffed her feet. She offered her hand to Mrs. Johnson. "Sarah Brighton."

Mrs. Johnson smiled. "Really? The writer? I thought I recognized you from somewhere. I have your books."

Sarah smiled nervously. She always felt uncomfortable when people recognized her.

Mrs. Johnson laughed and pulled her closer in a motherly hug.

"So pleased to meet you, my dear. Call me Amelia. My husband is Burt. Come inside for a cup of tea. You're icy cold. My husband will walk you home in a moment."

Sarah hadn't noticed how cold she was until Mrs. Johnson mentioned it. Grateful, she followed the couple inside their warm home. Buddy liked them, so they had to be good people.

Their kitchen was cozy, with a coal stove and a small table with four chairs in the center of the room. Amelia Johnson handed her a large cup of tea, which immediately warmed her when she sipped it. Buddy lay chewing a bone at her feet

"Sarah, were you disturbed by the terrible sound earlier?"

Sarah nodded. "Do you know what it was? I was concerned someone might have been hurt, or it could be an animal in pain."

Burt Johnson nodded. "It can be unnerving when you're new to the area. It almost changed our minds about living here. Luckily it doesn't happen all that often. Every few months or so."

Sarah frowned. "So you don't know what causes it? Have you ever searched for a cause?"

Amelia handed her another cup of tea.

"We did, after the first few times it happened. However, we could never find anything. Strange, I know, but it can't be anything serious. There is another old gentleman who lives in the woods by himself, Mr. Thompson, but it's doubtful that he has anything to do with it. He is a recluse and hardly speaks to anyone, but he seems quite friendly. I heard a story that he lost his daughter years ago under tragic circumstances. Try not to let the occasional creepy noises ruin your impression of the place. We love living here."

Sarah yawned after finishing her tea, and Burt got to his feet.

"Let me walk you home, my dear. You need a good night's sleep. It sounds like the noise has died down. Usually, once it goes away, you won't hear it again on the same night. Try to keep your dog inside when the noise should come again. You don't want him to run away and end up in the lake. The terrain can be treacherous. He seems like a good old fellow."

It turned out that she lived closer to the Johnsons than she had initially thought. Although she valued her privacy, it was comforting to know that there was someone close to her. She thanked Mr. Johnson profusely for getting her home safely. Sarah locked up the house securely and patted Buddy, who settled on the couch. She went to bed and slept straight through until the next morning.

Chapter 2: The Lake

After breakfast, Sarah decided to explore. She knew she should probably finish unpacking and get the house sorted out, but she wanted to get out into nature. She still felt cooped up from the long drive from the previous day. She could see Buddy was also anxious to get exercise.

She fed Buddy his chicken, which he swallowed in two bites, and then they walked down to the lake. It took her a while to get there, but she enjoyed the exercise. Buddy ran ahead, and she followed him through the trees. The terrain was rough, and one of her feet got tangled in the undergrowth. She almost fell, but stopped in time to pull herself free carefully. The lake was a surprise to her, as she hadn't been expecting it to be so beautiful.

The lake looked serene, surrounded as it was by towering trees and other lush greenery. People paid a lot of money to go on holidays in places like these. The lake's surface was like a mirror that reflected the surrounding beauty. As she walked closer to the lake, she wondered exactly how deep it was. The water appeared emerald green near the shore and a more sapphire blue in the deeper sections. She felt a strong pull to go swimming in the sapphire blue section and imagined holding her breath before diving down into the depths. There was a strong breeze in the air that made ripples dance over the lake's surface.

Sarah closed her eyes for a moment to appreciate the smell of damp soil, moss, and a sweet, flowery fragrance. She felt a sudden strange urge to become part of the beautiful environment.

Buddy barked, and she opened her eyes again to follow him down the wooden dock that stretched out into the lake. A boat was tied to the dock. It appeared to be in good condition, and she decided to take it out to do some exploring. She wanted to see if she could determine how deep the lake actually was.

She untied the boat and helped Buddy to jump into it. Sarah took the paddle and started steering the boat to the middle of the lake. Buddy watched her work for a while, and then he settled down and went to sleep. Sarah stopped steering the boat and just let it drift, enjoying the beautiful nature around her. She sighed and leaned against the side of the boat, enjoying the feel of the sun beating down on her skin.

She must have been sitting that way for barely two minutes when a sudden cold breeze disturbed her reverie. Surprised, Sarah opened her eyes. The weather had started to change. She didn't think she had ever experienced such a rapid weather change before.

The sky was turning gray, and the caressing rays of sunlight were disappearing behind the clouds that rapidly converged over the lake. Where had they come from? She hadn't even noticed their initial approach.

Buddy also seemed disturbed by the sudden change as he looked up and howled. Sarah was just thinking that she should steer them back to the shore when she saw the movement among the trees. Buddy must have seen it too, because he barked, sharp and high, as if he was anxious about whoever or whatever was moving around among the trees not far from them. At least they were out of reach on the water, if there was something in the woods. Unless it was something that could swim...

Sarah swallowed. Her throat had gone completely dry and her mouth was parched. She hadn't brought anything to drink with her, as she hadn't planned on being away from home for long. She tried to pull herself together. She had clearly been watching too many cheap horror movies.

It might even be the Johnson couple taking a walk down to the lake, or even the elderly gentleman who they said lived close by in the woods. She would wave at them when she saw them. She kept expecting the Johnsons to step out from the trees, but nobody came.

There was more movement, and the leaves on the trees rustled. However, nobody emerged from the woods. By now, Sarah also realized it was unlikely that the strange effects could be caused by people moving around. It was exceptionally fast and seemed to be all around them.

Buddy howled. She could see he didn't like what was happening at all. She knew there must be a rational explanation, but it was unlike anything she had ever seen before. For a moment, she again thought she could see figures moving around among the trees, but she quickly realized she must be mistaken.

Sarah decided to wait before taking the boat back to the shore, as she didn't understand what was happening. The movement hadn't stopped and instead seemed to be getting faster. It was stirring up a wind that was blowing out over the lake. It pulled at the boat and rocked it.

Buddy growled, and his hair stood on end. She patted his head.

"Just hold on, Buddy. I'm making sure it's safe. We're just going to have to stay still for a while."

Buddy calmed down and looked up at her with trusting eyes. She could feel the wind getting stronger, and the boat was starting to rock more. Above them, the sun was completely gone, and rain was starting to fall in big drops at first, and then poured down. Buddy howled and tried to make himself as flat as possible in the bottom of the boat, but soon they were both soaking wet.

Sarah couldn't see any more movement on the shore, and the wind had died down somewhat. She picked up the paddle with the intention of going back to the shore. The rain was icy cold, and she shivered. It was when she put the paddle into the water that a spine-chilling moan came from the woods. It wasn't the high-pitched keening from the previous night, but a much deeper groan. It sounded like someone had been in incredible pain for a long time.

Sarah leaned forward to try to see what was happening in the woods, and a hard gust of wind hit her from behind, overturning the boat and pitching her into the water with the paddle still in her hand. She heard Buddy yelp as he fell into the water before the boat hit her against her head as she went down. The pain made her see stars and pulled her deeper down into the lake. Sarah lost consciousness, and her mouth opened as water filled her lungs.

***

The world went gray before her eyes, but as she tried to focus, she found herself standing on the wooden dock next to the lake, watching a woman run toward her from the woods. Behind the woman, the trees were coming alive. White, smoky shapes swirled through them, creating a strong wind as they moved around furiously.

Sarah knew someone was chasing the woman, but she couldn't quite see who it was. It was a large, dark figure with no clearly visible features. She wanted to run, but she was frozen in place as she watched the nightmare unfold in front of her.

The woman was almost on the sand next to the lake when she opened her mouth, and that high-pitched keening Sarah had heard the night before came out. Sarah put her fingers in her ears to block out some of the sounds. The woman's face was frozen in a terrified rictus as she continued to produce the noise with great force.

She ran straight at Sarah, who wanted to get out of the way, but found that she still couldn't move. When the woman came closer, Sarah could see that she was dead, and had been for some time. Her dead eyes bulged out of her head, the flesh around them having rotted away a long time ago. Her mouth was open and a black substance bubbled from it.

Nevertheless, the woman was running fast, not stumbling like a zombie in a horror film. She fell before she could reach the dock and sprawled in the sand next to the water. When she went down, Sarah could see that there was a knife in her back. The dark figure that had been chasing her had never emerged from the woods.

The dead woman turned on her side in the sand and started writing with her finger. Sarah wanted to see what she was writing, but found she couldn't move. It felt as if the woman was taking forever to write one letter. An "H," "E," and then an "L" slowly formed in the sand.

Sarah thought she could hear Buddy barking somewhere behind her, but she couldn't turn her head to see where he was. Finally, the woman appeared to have finished her message, and she sat down on the sand. She looked around her, as if she didn't know where she was. A man came running from the woods with a long knife in his hands. He was a chunky young man, but he looked strong, and his eyes looked furious, with bushy eyebrows above them that made him look even more dangerous. The woman saw him coming, but she didn't move. Sarah got the distinct impression that she was too tired to move. She had given up and couldn't fight back anymore. Maybe the woman felt like she had felt when she left Josh—as if she was losing the will to live.

Sarah read "HELP ME" and shivered. The young man had now reached the woman, and she turned her face up to him and gave him a pleading look. The man slashed at her and drove the long knife into her body. The woman coughed and vomited up blood. She fell back on the sand with a large bloodstain spreading under her. Horror-struck, Sarah continued to watch the long-ago scene unfold in front of her. It gradually faded out, and it felt unreal, like she had been watching a movie scene.

She heard Buddy bark again, and this time she could turn around to look for him. Buddy bounded out of nowhere and jumped on her, causing her to fall back and hit her head on the wooden dock. The world grayed out, and when she came to herself again, she was spluttering in the water and fighting for air. She was confused, and then realized what she had seen must have been caused by oxygen starvation.

The boat was floating upside down next to her, but she couldn't quite reach it and felt herself going under again. Her fingers scraped on the boat's rough surface as she tried to hold on.

Then Buddy was next to her, and he grabbed the sleeve of her shirt, pulling her. She knew he wouldn't be able to save her, because she was simply too heavy, and her water-logged clothes were making her even moreso. She fought for air, but the darkness finally dragged her down, and she passed out.

***

The next time Buddy's barking woke her up, she found herself next to the lake with the boat in the shallow water near her. Buddy was going hysterical, and she could even see teeth marks on her arm where he had tried to drag her.

This time, she made sure that she was really on land, and not simply having another hallucination. She pinched herself, and a large red mark appeared on her arm. Her head was sore, and she felt fortunate to be alive, but she had no idea how long she had actually spent in the water. When she looked next to her in the sand, she almost choked. The vague outlines of the letters "H", "L", "P" and "M" were still visible.

Her head was sore, and her legs were shaky when she finally managed to stand up. She walked home, where she intended to spend the rest of the day unpacking. However, she was so tired that she fell on her bed and went to sleep. The incident at the lake had sapped all her energy.

She slept until nightfall without dreaming, and was only woken up by Buddy's barking when he wanted food. Sarah fed Buddy, and then went straight back to bed, as she was still struggling to keep her eyes open. Buddy settled in for the night next to her bed. She wanted to berate herself for not being productive, but then the move had been tiring, and she had had the accident at the lake. Besides, tomorrow was another day.

Sarah closed her eyes and dreamed. The girl was again running through the woods, being relentlessly chased by her unnamed and invisible assailant. However, this time the person who was chasing her was slowly becoming visible.

Sarah shuddered as she recognized the familiar face that was now a grimace of pure hatred. Josh was carrying a knife in his right hand, which he had lifted in an arc and was aiming at the young woman's back. For a moment, the woman's face turned into her own terrified face.

The woman tried to run faster, but Josh always stayed right behind her, even when she managed to run faster. The woman once more opened her mouth to scream for help, but no words came out, only a high-pitched keening sound.

The woman ran even harder, and for a moment Sarah was hopeful that she was going to outrun Josh. However, he jumped, and the knife sliced into the woman's back. The jogger fell down on her knees, and Josh was on her back, choking her with his hands, just like he had done to Sarah.

Sarah woke up in a cold sweat as the sun peeked in through the curtains she'd hung the day before.

Buddy barked for his breakfast and twirled in an excited circle when he saw her going to the kitchen.

Sarah made herself cereal and then realized she would have to go into the general store in town, as her cupboards were empty. All she really had in the way of groceries was the leftover food she had brought along from Josh's apartment.

Josh... She shuddered when she thought about him killing the girl in the dream. She didn't know if he had tried to contact her, because she had blocked his number on her phone. She hoped he wasn't looking for her, and that she hadn't left behind any evidence that could potentially help him find her. She had left a detailed letter behind, explaining why she was doing what she was doing. Sarah could imagine his face when he read the letter and then tore it into small pieces. Knowing Josh, he might have even eaten the pieces.

She hadn't wanted to hurt Josh, even though he had hurt her enough. He simply didn't care, even though he usually pretended afterward that he was sorry. Her therapist had told her that was something she had to work on: prioritizing her own needs and desires above those of the other people in her life. She was still finding this difficult, but she was doing her best to put herself first.

Buddy barked excitedly when she took out the car keys, and he ran in circles around her, almost causing her to fall on her way to the car.

Chapter 3: The Store

The town was a long drive away from the woods, and she wanted to buy sufficient stock so that she wouldn't have to go there again soon. Sarah had wanted to get away from civilization, and part of that involved not spending too much time in the shops. She also planned on starting a vegetable garden. She would have to fence it off, as she could imagine Buddy digging up the vegetables and eating them. He was a strange dog who sometimes seemed to prefer vegetables above meat.

As she wound her way through the narrow mountain road, the landscape became breathtaking. Rugged mountain faces adorned with verdant foliage towered over her on all sides as she drove. Being this close to nature just made her feel better in general.

The sound of the gravel crunching under the tires of her car created a soothing rhythm as she drove. When she looked in the mirror, she saw that Buddy had fallen asleep in the back seat. He was snoring gently, and his legs were twitching as if he was changing rabbits in a dream.

The road became extremely narrow at one point, and her anxiety kicked in. It felt as if her car was only clinging precariously onto the road, and she was afraid for a moment that it would fly off the next corner she came around, dashing her and Buddy to their deaths below. It was a steep drop, and she wondered how many people had died on this road.

She swallowed and forced herself to count to 10. That helped her overcome her fear, at least somewhat. When she drove into the little town, the main road was empty. She thought this was strange for a weekday. If it was a Sunday, she would have expected people to be at home, enjoying time with their families, but on a Tuesday, she had expected to see more people out and about, doing their shopping and going about their general business.

She stopped in the parking lot of the general store where she could only see two other cars. The place was clean in an almost clinical way. She was used to being harassed by beggars and seeing rubbish in the streets, but in this town, there wasn't a thing out of place.

Buddy yelped when she stopped the car. She didn't want to take him with her, as she wasn't sure how he might react to all the new people.

"Stay, Buddy. I won't be long."

She left the window slightly open for him. It didn't look like anyone was around who would want to steal a car. She saw Buddy staring after her as she entered the shop, and she gave him a little wave. She hoped the shop had his favorite snacks.

The clerk at the general store nodded at her when she walked in. She noticed that he was staring at her with a frown and that his eyes had widened slightly. Almost as if he had seen or met her before, but he couldn't remember exactly where. The cash register was so close to the exit that it would be almost impossible to sneak past him without paying. She assumed that was his intention. The store clerk was an elderly gentleman with thick, bushy eyebrows. He had a sturdy figure, and she thought he might be able to take on a much younger man in a fight. Sarah wondered if perhaps he was also the store owner, and that the actual clerk was ill or had taken leave. It seemed unusual for a person his age to be working as a clerk, but then, jobs were probably scarce in this area.

The shop had most of what she wanted but was short of some of her favorite items. She realized she would have to drive further out, at least at times, to get what she needed.

The clerk took his time to ring up her items. He frowned while he worked, and he was uncommunicative. He seemed cold, but she thought that maybe he was just introverted. She decided she might as well introduce herself and see what information about the woods she could get from the man.

"I'm Sarah Brighton, I bought the house close to the woods. It's a pleasure to meet you. Have you lived here a long time?"

The man nodded. "Aye, pleased to meet you. I'm Gerald McKenzie. I've lived in the area for the last thirty years or so. I run the store. I inherited the place from my late father. The store clerk, Tommy, is either ill or drunk. The boy has a drinking problem, so you're never sure about him. I need to fire him, but it's difficult to find someone else for the pay I can offer. The store hasn't been doing well over the last few years. There are simply too few people who live in this area. Most of the younger people have moved away. So, how do you like it up there? Lovely place, isn't it?"

Sarah smiled, delighted that she could get the man to communicate with her.

"The house is fantastic, and the woods are so beautiful, but I have noticed some strange things. I'm not sure if a lot of it is my imagination. I'm a writer, after all. A horrific noise came from the woods on my first night here. I've also seen movement in the woods, and I've felt a strong wind at times, as well as a lingering mist. I don't know if all these could just be natural weather effects. I've never lived so close to the woods."

The old man shook his head.

"Be careful up there, Ms. Brighton. I stay out of those woods myself. I've heard stories of people disappearing and never being found. A young lady disappeared a few years ago, never to be seen again. I believe they searched for her, but the terrain is rough in some places."

Sarah swallowed. "Eh, thanks for the warning. I'll keep that in mind."

When she carried her groceries out to the car, Buddy was trying to put his nose through the open part of the window. He wagged his tail and barked excitedly when he saw her.

She decided to drive through the rest of the town to see if there was anything that would interest her, but there didn't appear to be anything much happening. There was a restaurant, a small coffee shop and a library, but all of them were still closed. It was already 11 a.m. in the morning, so she couldn't help but wonder if they would open at all. It really seemed like a ghost town.

She drove past one other car going out of town. Well, she wanted to live in a quiet, peaceful place, and she seemed to have gotten what she wanted.

The drive back was uneventful, and she felt as if she was becoming more used to the road. She didn't feel any more as if she would fall to her death around every corner she took.

At home, Buddy ran in and out of the trees close to the yard while she unpacked the groceries. He seemed to realize that he would get into trouble if he ran off alone.

"Hey, Buddy! Do you want to go for a walk?"

The dog wagged his tail when he heard the word "walk."

Sarah packed herself a picnic lunch and some snacks for Buddy. She put on her hiking boots, even though she probably wouldn't be doing any hectic climbing, as she usually preferred to stick to the walking routes. She also put on her big, flowery hat to protect her face against the sun. Buddy barked at her, and she had to laugh. She wondered if the dog remembered that Josh had given her the hat.

Chapter 4: The Hike

The walk into the woods ended up taking her much longer than she initially thought it would. There were winding little paths everywhere that ended up in unexpected places.

The sun that shone above them created patches of light and warmth on the forest floor, which Buddy chased after. The labrador was behaving like a puppy again, barking at birds and chasing insects through the grass. She almost fell over him a few times.

Sarah felt herself gradually relax the further they walked into the forest. Part of the reason why she wanted to go for a long walk was also to clear her mind. She felt like she needed to figure out how she wanted to approach her career and the rest of her life. She had bought the house to get away from Josh, but she needed to see what she wanted to do from here onward. Her last two books were still selling well, and she had another half-completed novel. She hadn't worked on it much for the last few months, as she had been increasingly distracted as the situation between her and Josh deteriorated. She knew she needed to contact her agent, as her email inbox was full of unanswered messages, and there were voicemails on her phone. She had left a message two weeks ago that she was taking time for herself and would contact them when everything was settled. However, she realized that she would have to do that soon, as they needed to set a release date for her new book.

Buddy stopped to drink water from a stream and then plunged into it. He splashed around, and when she put her hand into it, she found the water was icy cold.

They continued their walk, and Sarah could see it was getting later in the day by the way the foliage was starting to cast shadows on the forest floor. They would have to turn around soon, as she didn't want to be trapped out here at night.

The previous warmth of the sunlight was being replaced by an icy coldness that pricked her skin. The trees, which had initially looked inviting to her, were now starting to cast long, gnarled shadows that looked contorted and twisted.

It was time to turn around and go back. Sarah thought she saw movement from the corner of her eye, but when she looked again, there was nothing.

"Come, Buddy!"

Buddy was unwilling at first, but she gradually persuaded him with biscuit treats to follow her back. She realized she was going to have to put up a fence around the house so that she could let him run around without constantly worrying about him. The move out here seemed to have made him more stubborn, and the woods attracted him. Maybe she could even create a workspace for herself. It could be inspiring to work outside in the fresh air and sunlight.

Then, from the corner of her eye, she saw the movement again. Figures and shapes darted among the trees, vanishing before she could fully see them. The shadows around her became sinister shapes and forms, and she had to stop herself from running through the woods. If her foot became entangled in something, she could fall and die here. Nobody would ever know what had become of her, except if the Johnsons found her by accident.

It got colder quickly, and for a moment Sarah thought she could see Buddy's teeth chattering. His fur was standing on end, and he appeared unsettled. They didn't seem to be getting any closer to home, and then she realized with a sinking feeling that they must have made a wrong turn somewhere. They had walked deeper into the woods instead of out of them. Sarah was just about to sit down and cry when she saw a wooden cabin ahead of her. The mist, which she had observed during her first night in the forest, was already creeping around it, creating the impression that the cabin was floating slightly above the ground.

A man stood next to it, watching them. He stood so still that she didn't notice him at first. The man was extremely tall, and he was old.

His back was bent, and she could see he moved with great difficulty. He finally lifted his hand to wave at them, and she waved back.

Sarah continued walking straight to him, as the old man didn't seem threatening in any way, and she needed his help to find her way home. When she got closer, she could see that he was studying her through red-rimmed eyes. It was possible that, at his advanced age, he couldn't see very well.

"Mary?"

His voice was low and thick as if he had phlegm in his throat. Sarah thought he probably hadn't spoken to anyone in a long time.

"Excuse me? I'm Sarah Brighton, I moved into the house just outside the woods. I am so pleased to meet you. I'm sorry if we're disturbing you. My dog is well-behaved."

The old man looked confused for a moment and then offered her his gnarled hand in greeting. His skin was very dry, but his hand was warm, and the handshake firm.

"Oh, excuse me. I'm Mr. Thompson. It's just that you look so much like my daughter Mary. My mind is playing tricks on me. She disappeared years ago, out here in the woods. She went for a run one day and never came back. How silly of me, to think that you must be Mary. If she is still alive, she would be many years older than you. But I don't think she is. I think the woods took her. You must be careful, young lady."

Sarah shuddered. While the old man seemed friendly, the expression in his eyes was vacant and dead.

"I'm so sorry to hear about your daughter. I had a strange experience the other day. I fell off my boat in the lake and hit my head on the side. I must have blacked out for a little while, but during that time I had a vision of a woman running through the woods and being chased by someone. She asked me to help her by scrawling the letters in the sand. She was a dark-haired girl, probably around my age, dressed in running clothes."

The old man listened closely, and he nodded.

"It could be her. Mary was always running, even at times when others warned her to be careful, when there was flooding during winter, or when visibility was poor, such as late at night. Mary loved these woods. That's the only reason why I stayed on after she went missing. I feel there is still something of her in these woods. If I moved away, all would be lost, and she wouldn't have a place to come back to, if she still wanted to come home."

Sarah felt sorry for the old man, but she wanted to go home, as the shadows all around them had gotten even deeper.

"Sorry, Mr. Thompson, but I would like to get home before it gets too dark. We seem to have gotten somewhat lost on our way back. Could you please direct us to what would be the quickest way out of the woods?"

Mr. Thompson nodded. For a few moments she thought he wasn't going to say anything, but then he started to explain the route in his painstaking fashion. She thanked him before she turned around, but she wasn't sure if he even heard her. The old man was focused on the woods, as if he expected his daughter to come walking through the trees back to him, after all these years.

She turned around to wave at him, but he just continued to stare ahead of him, as if he didn't see her. It worried her that an elderly person who could be frail and possibly have dementia was living by himself in the woods, but she wasn't really sure what she could do about it, since she wasn't related to him. She would mention it to the Johnsons the next time she saw them. Maybe they would know what to do.

Chapter 5: The Phone Call

After she got home, she made a small barbecue outside. It was earlier than she thought it was. The darkness of the woods had just confused her. Buddy walked up and down next to the barbecue, licking his lips. She smiled at the dog.

"Patience, Buddy. You'll get your piece."

Her cell phone started ringing when she went to the kitchen to make a salad.

The phone flashed the name "Louise." Her publisher. She probably wanted an answer about when she would be receiving the new manuscript. Sarah sighed. She hadn't really thought about it and didn't feel like speaking to the woman, but it probably wasn't a good idea to avoid her any longer. Louise could just talk so much once she got started.

She pressed to answer.

"Louise?"

She could hear Louise's heavy breathing on the other side. Louise was almost 60, and heavy set. She was an excellent literary agent and well-connected. Sarah doubted that she would have been so successful without Louise's support. That's why she had to continue being nice to Louise, and she had also been a better mother to Sarah than her own had ever been.

"My girl, goodness, everyone is wondering what has become of you. I'm glad I finally got hold of you."

Sarah smiled at the receiver. She always had a feeling that whomever she was speaking to could see her face, and that she should be on her best behavior. She supposed it was the type of behavior that had been drilled into her as a child.

"Louise, I'm so sorry that you struggled to get hold of me. I have been busy. The move took longer to sort out than I first thought."

Louise cleared her throat. It sounded like she was eating something.

"Don't worry, Sarah. I'm not worried about the book, we can give you extra time if you need it. I'm just calling to, ah, warn you about something."

A cold shiver went down her spine.

"What is it, Louise?"

She could hear Louise sighing.

"It's Josh, Sarah. He's been here, asking questions about you, wanting to know where you went. He's telling people that you just left him behind without a warning, after all that he's done for you. It's a regular smear campaign, he's bad-mouthing you to as many people as possible. He's telling people that you're mentally unstable, you tried to kill yourself, and you attacked him. Josh is saying the police must find you, and that you should be admitted to hospital for observation. Unfortunately, he has convinced some people to believe him. He's even had an interview with one of the tabloids."

Sarah dropped the knife she was going to use to cut the cucumbers and tomatoes.

"That doesn't surprise me. It sounds like him. I'm sorry that he's been hassling you, Louise."

Louise coughed. It worried Sarah that she sounded so out of breath. She was wheezing hard.

"Ah, don't worry about it, Sarah. I'm just glad you got away from him. I want you to look after yourself. I just thought I'd warn you. I didn't tell him anything about your whereabouts, but he's been sniffing about, trying to charm the girls in the office. They've all been warned not to tell him anything and not to get involved with him. My dear, I'm going to let you go. I need to run off to my next meeting."

Sarah said goodbye to Louise and hung up. She should have expected something like this, but it still worried her.

After supper, Sarah fell asleep in her rocking chair in the living room. A knock on one of the windows woke her up. She had always been a light sleeper and jumped straight out of her chair when she heard the knock.

Buddy also jumped up and ran at the window, barking at whatever it was he saw there.

Another knock came, this time from one of the other windows. Frantic, Sarah ran to the front and back doors, to make sure that she had locked them. Her heartbeat only slowed down somewhat when she saw she had indeed locked them.

A thumping sound came from the roof, right above her head. Buddy growled, a low, menacing sound. The thumping became louder and louder, almost as if someone was walking on the roof.

Sarah went to the kitchen and picked up the bread knife. It was the only thing she could use for self-defense. When she got back to the living room, the sounds stopped. There was another knock at the window, and she stepped forward and pulled the curtain away.

She screamed and dropped the knife when she found a white face staring back at her. The ghost, or whatever it was, place its pale hand against the window. It was freezing cold outside, and the creature used its long white fingers to write words on the window.

Sarah watched, horrified, as the thing's face kept changing. Sometimes it was just a white blur, but then it would change into the face of the woman she had seen in her vision at the lake. The face did indeed look much like her own, and she realized that it must be Mary, the old man's daughter.

However, what could the girl want if she had been dead for so many years? The words "HELP ME" slowly appeared on the window.

As Sarah continued to look through the window, something even stranger happened. The ghostly shape of the girl twirled around and reached upward with her arms. It almost looked as if the girl was drowning. She was desperately trying to swim to save her own life, but someone kept pushing her down and holding her under the water.

Sarah shivered. She had thought the girl was stabbed to death, but what if she drowned? Maybe she was trapped here until the mystery of her death had been solved? Did she want her body to be found, so that her father could get peace by giving her a proper burial?

The girl's face started changing, as Sarah was thinking what she could possibly do to help her. The face melted and then reformed itself until it changed into that of a man. At first, she thought it was Josh again, but it was the face of a young man she had never seen before. This ghostly apparition laughed at her, and she could see black pools of hatred swimming in his eyes. The ghostly face threw itself at the window with such force, that it caused a crack and sent Sarah staggering backward. She tripped and fell into her rocking chair. When she looked up, she could see that the apparition had broken apart and was disappearing slowly, one silky wisp of mist at a time.

Sarah woke up when Buddy jumped on the chair, and they both fell backward.

Chapter 6: The Ghost

The next morning, Sarah paced her house with all the doors locked and the windows closed. Buddy had whined at the door for a while, but after she had given him food, he had lain down and gone back to sleep. She needed time to decide what she was going to do about her predicament.

She was becoming increasingly uneasy in the house and the woods. She had moved into the house hoping to rebuild her life and find peace and quiet, but instead, she found "drama on a whole new level," as Louise would say.

She wasn't going to let a ghost chase her away from this perfect place. The ghost wanted something, and she was going to find out what it was. Another walk through the woods would be needed. This time she would go prepared.

She first needed to go into town to buy supplies. Gerald McKenzie gave her a strange look when she entered his store. She assumed the store clerk was still out of commission or had possibly been fired.

"Back so soon?"

She smiled at the old man. "Yes, I just need a spade and a few knives. I don't have much in the way of cutlery, you know."

Gerald McKenzie frowned. "Planning to do gardening, are we? The soil up there isn't great, but I suppose you could give it a try. It's always handy to have some extra steak knives."

Sarah smiled sweetly. She really didn't like the way the man was looking at her. It was strange, but the previous time she hadn't found him so creepy.

"Not gardening, not exactly. But I might have to do quite a bit of digging. So you know there's a ghost up there? I've seen her; it's a girl with long dark hair."

Mr. McKenzie looked at her with a puzzled expression.

"A ghost? Oh dear... young lady, don't you think it's too isolated for you up there? Maybe you need more companionship."

Sarah thanked the old man for her purchases and then walked out, not looking back. Clearly, he thought she was crazy.

While she was driving home, Buddy got restless in the car. She had been thinking of how she could contact the ghost and persuade her to go with her to find the remains. Much as she was scared of the apparition, Sarah thought this might be the only solution. If she received a proper burial, her spirit might be able to move on to the next life.

Buddy wouldn't stop barking, and when she finally looked over her shoulder, she saw the vague outline of a woman sitting in the back seat. She turned back quickly to watch her driving, as she knew she was coming up to a sharp corner. She was still nervous of the ghost, but she was fairly certain it wouldn't do anything to her.

Buddy had stopped barking, and she could only persuade herself to look into the backseat again when she was closer to home. The ghost was still there and now appeared more solid. It was looking straight ahead, and she thought it was smiling at her. Buddy was now regarding it with curiosity more than anything else. He pawed at it, and his foot went straight through its middle.

When Sarah stopped the car at home and opened the back door to let Buddy out, the ghost was gone. For a few moments, she thought it was entirely possible that she was losing her mind. She had experienced almost non-stop stress for the last few months of her life, so anything was possible.

She turned to Buddy.

"How do we get her back, Buddy? We need her to show us how we can help her."

Sarah took a beer out of the fridge and tried to remember what she had been doing in the car when she could get the ghost to appear to her. She sat down in her rocking chair and took some large gulps from her beer. She had been thinking about how to contact the ghost, and then the spirit had appeared to her...

Sarah closed her eyes for a few moments, and when she opened them, the ghost was standing next to her. She nearly dropped her beer on the floor. The ghost was becoming increasingly clear. It seemed each time Sarah saw her, she could identify more details.

"Good, eh, Mary? I assume you're Mary? I'm pleased to meet you. I've met your father—lovely man."

The ghost nodded.

Sarah put the beer down and got up to retrieve the spade and two of the knives. She was wearing her swimsuit under her clothes in case she had to dive.

She could feel the icy coldness the ghost carried around with her when she moved around her back. Sarah didn't really know how ghosts made themselves visible. She hoped Mary wasn't using all her energy to make sure Sarah could see her. Their mission would be a failure if she ended up disappearing.

As Sarah walked through the woods with Buddy running after her, she noticed the ghost appearing, and then disappearing. She wondered what the ghost would tell her if she could speak.

When the ghost stayed away for a long time, she called her name.

"Mary! Can you show me where you are?"

The ghost didn't reappear for a long time, and Sarah wondered if she had used all the energy she had. The strangeness of the situation struck her, and she thought what a good story it would make. Nobody would believe her. It would be totally unlike the romantic stories she normally wrote.

The ghost floated ahead of her and pointed through the trees at the water.

"What is it? Is your body in the water? Did he drown you?" Sarah looked back, but the ghost was gone.

She waited for her to come back, but this time the ghost seemed to have disappeared for good. Sarah walked up and down next to the lake, but nothing further happened. It was almost as if the ghost felt that she didn't have to create scary effects now that she had Sarah's attention.

Sarah considered taking the boat out onto the lake, but she wasn't sure what that would achieve. Finally, she turned around and started walking home.

On the way back, she ran into Mr. Johnson. He was dressed in his hiking boots and used a walking stick. He looked serious and concerned, very much unlike the man she had met on her first night in the woods. From his expression and gestures, she immediately guessed that something bad must have happened.

"Sarah! There you are. We were concerned when we got to your house and there was nobody there. One of your windows is also cracked. Did you know about that?"

She nodded. It was where the ghostly figure had rammed itself into it the previous night, but she was obviously not going to tell him that.

"Uh, I had an accident when I was playing around with Buddy. I ended up falling against the window. Stupid of me, but at least it didn't break."

Mr. Johnson nodded, but she could see his mind was elsewhere.

"Is something wrong?"

Mr. Johnson nodded again, and she thought it looked as if he was scared of something. He kept looking over his shoulder.

"I shouldn't have left my wife behind, but what could I do? I didn't want her to see that. I told her to stay in the house and lock the doors and windows."

Sarah got an uneasy feeling in her stomach.

"Mr. Johnson, what are you talking about? What happened?"

He grimaced, and for a moment she thought he was going to cry.

"Young lady, I'm glad you weren't there to see it. It turned my stomach, it truly did. Who would do something like that to an old man?

What did the old fellow ever do to anyone? He lived there, out of the way, waiting for his lost daughter to return. You know, I spoke to him about a month ago, and he still thought she was going to return to him one day. I think his mind was starting to wander. He didn't seem that lucid anymore."

Sarah shivered. She realized he was talking about old Mr. Thompson. She touched Mr. Johnson's arm gently in an attempt to get him to focus on the present time.

"Mr. Thompson? Is he... Is he dead?"

Mr. Johnson nodded, biting his lip.

"It's the most disturbing thing I've seen. I'm telling you...Someone beat the old man to death. If he was bludgeoned, his assailant must have hard hands and immense strength. Never stopped hitting the poor old man. And it happened recently. It must have been earlier today. I have called the police, but it will take them some time to get here. They have to come from the next town, which is miles away. That's why I thought I would check on you. I wanted to warn you. I got quite worried when I didn't see you around."

Sarah went cold. Was that why Mary's ghost had disappeared so suddenly?

"I will go home, and lock myself in the house until the police come. We will be fine."

Mr. Johnson nodded. "That is probably the safest thing to do. We don't know if the murderer might still be around. The police will search the area. Let me walk you home so that I can assure myself you'll be safe. Then I'll go home to my wife."

On the way home, Sarah didn't see the ghost again. She waved at Mr. Johnson as he left, after she locked herself in the house as she had promised she would.

Chapter 7: The Dream

The police didn't show up until the late afternoon. She could see them moving through the trees around her house. They knocked on her door, and she answered their questions as well as she could. She told them about meeting Mr. Thompson in the woods, and that he had been a friendly and helpful old gentleman. She told them what she knew about the disappearance of his daughter. Sarah never said anything about the ghost, as she knew they wouldn't believe her, and that they might think there was something wrong with her. Josh had already created that impression about her in the media.

One of the policemen had already looked at her askance. As the others were leaving her house, he stayed behind to talk to her.

"You're the writer lady, aren't you? The one who ran away from her boyfriend? I saw an article about you. He said you were..."

One of the older men walked back and pulled him away.

"Stop that nonsense, Bill. It has nothing to do with us. Sorry, Ms. Brighton, for the interference. Bill here tends to get carried away. He's still new to the force."

Sarah nodded. "Don't worry about it. No offense taken."

She saw the young policeman looking back at her, as they walked away from her house. She couldn't help but wonder what else Josh had been saying about her to the press.

***

Sarah was eager to get out of the house and to start looking for Mary's remains, but it was too late by the time the police had finished searching the area. She made herself some soup on the small stove she had brought with her and gave Buddy his pellets. He gave her an annoyed look as if he wanted to ask why he was getting this and not fresh meat.

She made herself a cup of warm milk and then settled into her rocking chair with a book. She often found it difficult to finish a book and usually ended up reading several at once. Sarah often looked for books that could inspire her to come up with innovative ideas for the book she was writing at the time, but it was difficult, as she tended to be fussy. She had an entire collection of books in paperback she hadn't read yet, as well as several books she had downloaded onto her Kindle. What had been happening to her over the last few weeks had also completely distracted her, and she hadn't written a word.

After a while, she felt herself losing interest in the book. Her eyelids started drooping. She often found she stayed awake longer if she read books on her Kindle, but it wasn't charged at the moment.

Sarah fell into a deep sleep. She dreamed she was walking through the woods, barefoot, without Buddy. Ahead of her, she saw two white shapes flitting in the night. The one was Mary because she saw dark hair floating above the ghostly figure. Next to her was another ghost, whose fingers were intertwined with Mary's. She followed the ghosts on their path through the woods, for a long time. Soon, they came to Mr. Thompson's cabin, which she instantly recognized.

The ghosts half-turned to her, and she recognized that the other ghost was Mr. Thompson, as she had initially thought. They both pointed to the house in front of them as if they wanted to focus her attention on the scene that was about to unfold.

A man was knocking on the cabin's door. Mr. Thompson was still very much alive in this vision. He opened the door, roared in anger when he saw who it was, and instantly knocked the man over. Sarah watched, shocked at what was taking place right in front of her. The man was back on his feet almost immediately and smacked Mr. Thompson down with a strong backhand. Sarah couldn't make out who the man's assailant was. Mr. Thompson was screaming at the man, who kept beating and pushing him. She was surprised to find that she could hear the exact words of what he was screaming at the other man, even though she still couldn't make out who the assailant was. Mr. Thompson in the scene in front of her was wheezing badly now, but she could still hear what he was saying. She wanted to help him and had to remind herself that what happened was already in the past, and there was nothing she could do to help the poor man. In a sense, this scene was a ghost as well. The area had captured an impression of what had happened and was now showing it to her.

"It was you! I should have known! It was always you! The way you ran after her and followed her everywhere! You killed my Mary! Nothing—*ah*!—can bring her back."

Mr. Thompson kept screaming these words, until he collapsed on his knees, beaten, bloody, and bruised. He finally succumbed to a brutal kick in the head. His body was still, and he didn't move again after that.

Sarah started crying at the brutality the poor man had to suffer. He didn't deserve to die in such an awful way. When she turned around to speak to the ghosts, they were both gone.

Sarah woke up in her rocking chair, crying and gasping. Buddy was staring at her with wide eyes.

"Oh, Buddy, what are we going to do?"

She got up to make herself a cup of tea with several spoonfuls of sugar in it. Sugar always calmed her nerves, and she was feeling very rattled. After a while, she felt calmer and went to her bedroom to see if she could get some more sleep. She knew she had to somehow resolve the situation; otherwise, she would never find peace. However, she was too tired to focus on anything and spent the rest of the night in a dreamless sleep.

Chapter 8: The Search

When Sarah woke up the next morning, her entire body was sore, and she had a headache. She felt like spending the day in bed, but she knew she had to get up and deal with what was happening around her, otherwise; she was just going to end up feeling worse. The situation would also continue to worsen if it wasn't dealt with, now.

She made herself a bowl of cereal and opened the front door so that Buddy could go out to do his business and run around the house. While she ate, she thought about her ability to see the ghosts, and what it meant. People would call her crazy, especially after what Josh had told the newspapers.

She remembered seeing ghosts as a child and speaking to them. Her dead grandmother had come to her shortly after she passed away and had given her important information she had to give to the rest of the family. The family had first looked at her strangely, but when she started giving them facts that only her grandmother knew, they believed her.

"Right Buddy, I think we need to get up and get going. Don't ask me precisely what we're going to do, I only know we need to do something."

Sarah packed a flask of coffee, sandwiches, the spade, and two knives. She still wasn't sure why she needed the knives, but something was telling her to take them.

She locked the house behind her and set off into the woods, with Buddy chasing butterflies around her feet.

She didn't expect to see the ghosts again so soon after what had happened the day before, and the day was so bright and sunny that it seemed unlikely they would make themselves visible. The previous experience she had with ghosts told her that they preferred nighttime and cloudy days.

However, she was wrong. She hadn't gone far when she saw Mary's ghost coming toward her. She didn't see Mr. Thompson's ghost and noticed that Mary looked sadder than usual. Maybe Mr. Thompson had moved on, while Mary still had unfinished business.

"Mary, are you going to help today? If you help me, I can help you be at peace."

She looked at the ghost, who made a pleading face at her and then disappeared. Sarah put the spade over her shoulder and started walking toward the lake.

It was nice down at the lake, and Sarah decided to go for a swim. She took the boat out and put her clothes down next to her. Buddy had decided to stay on land today. When she indicated that he should jump into the boat, he just howled and ran away.

Sarah jumped into the water. It was refreshing after being on the boat in the warm sun for a while. She wondered how deep the lake was. She was a good swimmer, but she didn't think she would be able to dive all the way down to the bottom. It was dark and deep with strands of weeds reaching upward.

It was as if something was pulling her down into the dark depths of the lake to investigate. For a moment, she felt sure that the key to what she was searching for was there in the deep, dark depths.

Sarah treaded water for a few moments, trying to decide what to do. There was no one around who could help her surface if she got into trouble. After what had happened the other day, she was also wary. She still wasn't quite sure how she managed to get to the shore.

She didn't see Mary, and after a few more moments, she decided to dive down. The water was cold and dragged at her limbs. When Sarah looked up, she could still see light above her. She felt like she should go back to the boat, but for some reason, she felt compelled to dive even deeper.

At the bottom of the lake, she could see white bones gleaming. A human skull was lying close to her, and she reached for it. When she tried to pull it back, the thing was impossibly heavy, and she couldn't lift it. Sarah pushed it away from her but found that her fingers were stuck inside its mouth, almost as if the skull was trying to bite them off. Panicking, she started swimming upwards with the heavy thing still pulling her down. Her lungs already felt as if they were about to burst. She managed to move a little bit before she was pulled back down. Sarah fought against the skull, but then she saw Mary's face floating before her face. Mary looked sad. Sarah opened her mouth, and the water started flooding into her lungs.

Suddenly, the pressure on her hand was gone, and she was pushed from below. Sarah was shocked into wakefulness and closed her mouth. She looked down to see that Mary was pushing her. When they got near the surface, Mary disappeared, and Sarah had to swim up the rest of the way herself. She was weak, but she managed to lift herself out onto the boat, where she started coughing up water. She hung over the side and watched Buddy run up and down, barking like crazy on the shore.

When she felt slightly better, Sarah started paddling back to the shore. She started shaking when she put her feet down in the sand. Buddy ran to her and started licking her hands.

She was going to have to find a way to remove Mary's bones from the lake. That seemed to be easier said than done. She was convinced the girl's spirit would be able to pass over if she could give her a decent burial. Sarah walked back to her house with the spade over her shoulder and Buddy running after her.

The rest of the day and the evening were quiet. It was probably the quietest it had been since she moved here. Sarah took the time to read and play with Buddy. She cooked a stew and answered some emails and text messages that she hadn't had the time to respond to. Several of her friends mentioned that they had read Josh's interview in the press and that they hoped she was finally finished with him and doing well on her own.

The quiet evening made her feel more at peace. This was what she wanted her life to be like when had she moved out here. However, she couldn't help but feel that this was just the calm before the storm.

Chapter 9: Found

The next three days were peaceful until she had to drive out to town because she was running out of supplies again. She also felt like getting out and seeing other people, even if it was only old Mr. McKenzie at the store. Maybe she could get more interesting information about the area from him. She went for tea with the Johnsons occasionally, but they had been quiet after the death of Mr. Thompson. She also didn't feel like bothering them and making a potential nuisance of herself.

She took some time to continue working on her book; after all, that was the real reason she had come out here. She wanted more time to spend on her writing in a peaceful environment.

When she entered the store, she was shocked by the changes in Mr. McKenzie's appearance. He looked much older and as though he felt sorry for himself. She saw that his one hand was in a cast, and there were bruises on his face.

"Oh dear, Mr. McKenzie, don't tell me you were attacked too? You've probably heard about Mr. Thompson in the woods. The poor soul was brutally murdered. I thought things like this don't happen on this side of the world."

Poor Mr. McKenzie could barely speak when he responded. She saw finger marks on the old man's throat where he had been throttled.

"It was a mugger who grabbed me just before I could get into my house. The fool isn't from here, have never seen his ugly face before. It's sad, isn't it, what the world is coming to? No respect for others, it's everyone for themselves. Unfortunately, I'm too old to fight back now, with all my health problems and all. If I'd been younger, I could have taught him a lesson."

After wishing Mr. McKenzie a speedy recovery, Sarah took her groceries and walked to her car. It would be nice to meet up with someone for a cup of coffee and a slice of cake somewhere, but the town was just as quiet as it always was.

When she pulled out of town, she saw a car driving behind her, the first one she had seen in a long time. She watched the car, but the windows were tinted and she couldn't determine if it was a man or woman who was driving it. It took another turnoff and then disappeared from her view.

Buddy barked at the car, and she thought that maybe he was also longing for company. Maybe it was time to get another dog, who could be a companion for Buddy, but also extra security. Sarah had always rather liked giant Schnauzers, since they were easy to train and made excellent companions.

"What do you say, Buddy? Do you need a brother or a sister?"

Buddy barked and wagged his tail at her.

"Hey, don't get all excited, yet. I need to do some research first. We might need to drive a long way to find you a brother."

***

When she got home, she sensed a presence around the house. Was it Mary or her father? Or possibly both of them? She had really hoped that Mr. Thompson at least had moved on. Everything was still as she had left it. Her house was locked, and all the windows closed.

Buddy sniffed around and then barked at her. He didn't seem to want to move from the spot where he was standing. She walked over to him and saw two footprints on the ground, close to the front door. The prints were quite large and looked like they could have been left by a man's running shoes. Possibly Mr. Johnson's prints. He had quite large feet, and the only shoes she ever saw him wear were running shoes.

She went inside to put her groceries away and then back outside to think and watch Buddy run around. Sarah thought that there must be a way to get Mary's remains to the surface of the lake without drowning herself in the process. She didn't understand what was preventing her from fulfilling her goal. Was it the fact that the murderer had never been caught? Sarah shuddered. She didn't have the ability to catch a murderer.

If only she had seen the face of the man who had killed Mr. Thompson, as it was clearly the same man who had also murdered his daughter. She felt as if some kind of evil energy was preventing the spirits from gaining peace. The evil energy had desecrated nature and was keeping them trapped here. Sarah smiled wryly when she thought about what Louise would say about her fertile imagination. She decided to go for another walk with Buddy, just to clear her mind.

She intended not to go too far from the house, but before she knew it, they were far past the lake again. She was feeling relaxed and started exploring the beautiful natural environment around her when Buddy suddenly started barking. She ignored him at first because it sounded like his normal, talkative bark. Sarah continued to smell the wildflowers she had picked and didn't turn around fast enough when she heard the footsteps behind her. She felt the pain in her leg before she saw him.

Josh was standing there, his face a rictus grin. He held a pistol in his hand.

Chapter 10: Josh

"What?"

She was too surprised to say anything coherent before the pain hit her.

"You... you shot me."

He grinned at her. She wouldn't have believed it before, that he was capable of something like this. She might have expected a slap or a kick, but never that he would actually be crazy enough—or have the guts—to use a gun on her.

"Did you really think you were going to get away from me? That I would just let you go, with all the money you owe me?"

She was flabbergasted. He was still pointing the gun at her, but the pain overwhelmed her senses, and she had to sit down. She sat down in the grass, and looked at the hole in her leg while he continued to point the pistol at her head. She could see it wasn't serious—it was more a flesh wound than anything—but she wasn't going to tell him that. It was bleeding profusely, and she was planning to use that to her advantage.

"That will teach you. If you end up dying, it's just your own fault. What were you thinking, that you could actually leave me, just like that? You threw me away like I'm just some old piece of rubbish."

She ignored his taunting. Sarah tore a piece of her shirt and wrapped it around her leg. Josh stood watching her, not saying anything. She could see his hand was shaking. Even when he had a gun, he was still a coward.

"What do you mean about the money I owe you, Josh? As far as I know, I don't owe you anything."

Josh laughed.

"Sure, that's what you would say. You helped pay for the house and the bills, but you're a much higher earner than I am. You're the up-and-coming author who is just going to get more famous, and richer. You owe me for the years we've been together. I made sacrifices, you know. All those parties I had to attend alone, while you were at home, writing. You made me look bad in front of my friends. Writing was always more important to you than I was. When people asked me where my girlfriend was, you were either typing on your laptop or stuck with your nose in a book."

She would have been amused if her life hadn't been in danger. Had she really been with such a ridiculous man for such a long time? Yet, she had been so scared of him, scared enough to run away and hide, like a thief in the night. However, she understood that she was still in danger.

"Where has your stupid dog gone? He was just there, barking at me, and now he's run off somewhere. If I see him again, I'm going to put a bullet through his brain. I could never stand that mutt. He almost tore me to pieces, and you didn't even care, Miss Goody Two-Shoes."

Sarah tried to push herself up into a standing position while she held onto the tree. He knew how much Buddy meant to her, and in the mood he was in at the moment, he would do anything to hurt her.

"Really, Josh, what do you want from me? Are you here to kill me? Do you think they wouldn't know it was you? Even now, you've taken things too far. This is already attempted murder. You didn't think this through, did you?"

For a moment, he looked shocked, and she hoped he would drop the pistol. However, he didn't.

"I want you... I want you to either take me back or to sign an agreement to pay me a portion of your earnings, going forward. Like alimony. Then I'll leave you alone. If you sign the papers, you'll never hear from me again."

Sarah frowned.

"But Josh, we've never been married, and you have a well-paying job. It's not like we even have children."

He flinched when she said that, and she saw another opportunity to weaken him.

"Oh, Josh... you didn't lose your job, did you? I've always told you to watch your mouth around your boss. She's not..."

Josh suddenly screamed and fired a shot into the air. She realized that she had taken things too far. She'd opened up a wound that had just started to heal.

"Shut up, woman! Or I kill you right here, on the spot."

Sarah lifted her hands in a motion of surrender.

"Okay, okay... I'm sorry. Did you bring the paperwork you want me to sign? Let's go back to my house."

Josh frowned at her.

"So, you're not willing to take me back?"

Sarah sighed. Josh was destroying her will to live. He had a unique ability to do that.

"Josh, you just shot me. Things hadn't been going well between us for a long time. If it will make you happy to leave me behind, and go out and create a new life for yourself, I will sign your paperwork."

She could see by the expression on Josh's face that he didn't trust her intentions.

"Well, okay then. Can you walk? Do I need to give you my arm?"

At first, she wanted to decline, but then she thought he was unlikely to shoot her as long as she went along with what he wanted. She grabbed Josh's shoulder, and they stumbled back to her house. There was still no sign of Buddy, which worried her. She prayed that they would run into Mr. Johnson on the way, but that didn't happen.

When they reached the house, Josh actually smiled, as if he was doing her the biggest favor in the world.

"See, everything will be fine, as long as you do what I tell you to do. There's no reason for anyone to get hurt. Give me your keys."

Her hand shook as she took the house keys from her pocket and handed it to him. He helped her inside, and locked the door behind them. She sat down on the couch, and he handed her the contract.

She was hopeful that she could end the situation in her favor until she started reading it. The paperwork he handed her was nonsensical, but she couldn't tell him that. As she turned the pages, she realized it was just complete nonsense that he had written himself. She thought she should just sign it to get rid of him, but it made her worried about his state of mind. What if he decided to turn the gun on her again? The entire document read like it had been written by someone who had lost his marbles.

She smiled. "This seems, ah, reasonable to me. So, can I just sign right here at the end, Josh?"

Josh frowned. "How do I know I can trust you? Are you going to go to the police about your leg?"

She shook her head. "No. I mean we were together for a long time, Josh. I think both of us just need to move on to a happier place in our lives. I don't have any bad feelings toward you."

Josh looked like he wanted to smile, but then he frowned. "Where is that dog of yours? I don't trust it."

She felt as if she wanted to scream, but she knew she had to keep on playing his game. "Buddy is just off playing somewhere. He loves exploring. He'll come back, he always does."

She thought Josh would finally put the gun down, but he walked to the door. "I'm just going to check on that dog. Something's not right here. You're trying to con me, somehow. It's been too easy to get you to sign that form."

She wanted to protest and to tell him that he'd been holding a gun against her head, so what did he expect, but she managed to keep quiet.

Josh unlocked the front door and stepped outside. Everything was quiet for about two minutes, and then all hell broke loose.

Chapter 11: The Fight

Sarah heard Josh scream, and then he fired the pistol. Panic struck her, and she hobbled to the door, certain she would find Buddy dead outside. Instead, she found Josh holding someone in a headlock, whom he pushed against a tree. He was still holding the gun and fired it again. The other man grunted as it hit him in the arm.

The man was heavier than Josh and appeared older. To her horror, she saw it was Gerald McKenzie from the store in town. She was about to scream at Josh to stop when Mary's ghost appeared next to her. Her face was very sad, and she pointed at Mr. McKenzie, who was still trying to escape Josh's grasp.

The old man was incredibly strong for his age. He threw Josh to the ground and pinned him there. The pistol was knocked from Josh's hand and fell close to her on the ground. Sarah reached out and grabbed it. Mary's ghost was still next to her, and now she could see Mary's father as well.

Mr. McKenzie still had Josh pinned to the ground, but he briefly looked in their direction. His eyes widened and she realized he could see the ghosts. He turned his gaze to Sarah, and his eyes were full of hatred.

"You! I know they told you what I did. I killed both of them, and they made me do it. Now I'll forever be doomed to hell, on account of them. That's why I came here, to kill you as well before you could go to the police. I'll bury your body out here before someone can find it. "

Sarah took a few steps backward. She needed to get away from them and lock herself in the house, but she still didn't know what Josh had done with the key. Her eyes frantically searched the ground in front of her.

McKenzie reached for her, but then Josh gave him a hard knock against the head. He fell, and Josh went to stand on him, pressing his foot into the man's chest.

Sarah saw the keys fall from Josh's pocket and jumped to grab them. However, Josh saw her intentions and also reached for them. Sarah managed to knock them out of his hand and put them in her pocket. Josh realized his mistake too late, as McKenzie grabbed his legs and pulled him over backwards. He fell hard and knocked his head against the tree.

As Sarah ran into the house, she saw Buddy run from among the trees. She was scared he would be drawn to the fighting men, but he ran right past them and into the house. She ran in after him and locked the door behind them.

She realized the men could break the windows, but they would be delayed. Sarah found her cell phone and pressed Mr. Johnson's number. He answered almost immediately.

"Hello, my dear, are you looking for us? We came to town to do some shopping, but now the grocery store is closed, can you believe it?"

Sarah explained to him what was happening, and that she needed his help. Mr. Johnson assured her that they would be there as soon as possible and that she should stay locked inside with her dog. He also said she shouldn't hesitate to use the pistol if she had to do so.

Sarah sat down next to the window and waited, with Buddy next to her. The bandage on her leg was getting soaked through with blood.

Outside her house, the fight continued. She could also see the two ghosts, father and daughter, appearing and disappearing close to the two fighters. It was almost as if they were watching the fight with as much anticipation as she was herself.

It looked like Josh had broken Mr. McKenzie's nose, but he was as brutal as ever. He hit Josh in the mouth with one of his big, blocky fists, and she saw an eruption of blood, as well as teeth being knocked from Josh's mouth. Sarah winced, but Josh screamed, and this injury seemed to make him angrier than ever. Berserk with anger, he jumped on old McKenzie and head-butted him. Mr. McKenzie staggered, and for a moment she thought he was going down, but he managed to maintain his balance.

She wondered what Josh was fighting for. Surely not for her, or to save her life, as he had almost killed her himself. Josh had a horrific temper, and she supposed McKenzie may have made him so angry by attacking him first that he was just fighting to avenge his own ego. Josh couldn't bear to lose to anyone. He was always right, and he had to win any form of competition. She thought it was almost like a type of road rage. Sarah had once seen him almost beat a man who had turned in front of them in the road.

He had to win at all costs and couldn't allow anyone to overpower him. When she looked back on their life together, she increasingly realized Josh had never cared about anyone but himself. She had thought of him as a coward, but here he was showing himself to have some backbone after all. He would stand up for himself at least.

Mr. McKenzie had a black eye, but the horrible old man was still full of life and ready for more fighting. Even his injured hand, with which he had probably killed Mr. Thompson, didn't hold him back. The hand was in a cast, and he was ramming the extra hardness into Josh's face. He was just an older, and slightly worse, version of Josh.

Josh was getting beaten to a pulp, but she found she didn't care. McKenzie was still in a marginally better condition. The more they took out their hatred on each other, the less of a problem they would be for her, or the Johnsons.

She wished the Johnsons were here, but she realized it would take them time to drive back. Sarah only hoped the two fighters would remain focused on each other during this time and not turn their attention to her. Hopefully, they would run out of steam by the time the Johnsons got to her house.

She had just considered that thought when the front window shuddered under Josh's weight as Gerald McKenzie threw him against it. Buddy barked hysterically as Josh seemed to bounce off it and then roll onto the ground. Sarah couldn't breathe. She wheezed in anxiety, but the window held. If the two unbalanced men were able to get into the house, she would be in serious trouble. Fortunately, the windows appeared strong, but she also realized that they wouldn't be able to withstand repeated attacks. From the way the two men continued fighting, she wondered if either or both of them had taken drugs. Their pain thresholds seemed incredibly high as they continued to beat each other mercilessly. She had suspected before that Josh might be taking drugs at times, but she could never find any evidence except his increasingly violent behavior. She certainly hadn't wanted to be in a long-term relationship with an abusive drug user.

The ghosts had disappeared. All the violence was too much for them. Sarah didn't know if she should laugh or cry. From the way things were going, she thought that one of the men, or both, would end up dead.

McKenzie looked as if he was slowing down, and she thought youth might win over age after all. He had fallen, and Josh was kicking him in the head. However, the old man made a comeback by grabbing Josh's legs and pulling him down. Josh fell, and she saw a terrible look of fury on McKenzie's bruised face. She briefly wondered if the old man had been a wrestler in his youth.

He got up and took Josh's head between his hands. Sarah's heart beat faster as she could see that Josh was too tired to keep fighting back. McKenzie was like an indestructible beast.

McKenzie twisted Josh's head on his neck, and she thought he would twist it right off Josh's body with his immense strength. She couldn't hear the sound of his neck breaking, but she instantly knew Josh was dead. He fell to the ground like a limp rag doll.

Sarah was completely shocked, her mind dull, but she knew that she would be the next target and that she would have to react. After all, McKenzie had admitted that he'd come out here with the purpose of killing her.

While McKenzie had won the fight, she could also see that he had been severely injured. The man could barely stand, but still, he came stumbling to her house. Sarah picked up Josh's pistol and prayed there were enough bullets left.

She would react when McKenzie reacted. As long as she was in the house with Buddy, away from him, she was safe. Her real problems would start when he found a way into the house.

McKenzie was like a bull who had seen red. Sarah was starting to feel like the mom and son who were stuck in their car in Stephen King's novel *Cujo* while they were being stalked by the crazed dog.

Mckenzie walked around the house, glaring at her. She felt he was trying to intimidate her. He bared his teeth, and she showed him the pistol. She expected that he would storm the house and try to kick the windows or door out, but instead, he disappeared from view.

Mary's ghost flashed into view for a moment and pulled a sad face at her. Sarah wanted to walk over to the window to get a view of what McKenzie was doing, but she knew she would be putting herself in danger.

Instead, she paced up and down in the living room, while Buddy ran around her feet and barked. She could see McKenzie walking back to the house, grinning through the blood that covered his face. Sarah thought if she was going to survive this day, she would have nightmares for the rest of her life. McKenzie was pointing at something that he was carrying, in his hands. He was piling up stones, including large rocks, next to the living room window. This wasn't going to end well, possibly for both of them.

When he had a pile in front of him, he stood back to admire his handiwork. Sarah clutched the pistol and walked through to the kitchen. Buddy followed her, and she locked the door behind them.

Just then, she heard the first rock hit the window. It didn't come through, not yet. Sarah took up position behind the kitchen door, pointing the pistol. She heard more crashes and glass breaking as he demolished the windows. Sarah heard the front door opening.

McKenzie must have put his arm through the window and opened it from the inside.

She knew she had to finish it before the Johnsons came back. She couldn't put them at risk as well. She heard a strange noise as he moved through the house. He was either whistling or singing some strange song to himself. The man was completely insane.

"Hello! Little girl, where are you? You don't want to be scared of me, I'll send you to be with your friends. Together, you can haunt these woods forever."

Buddy barked. It didn't really matter, though; the kitchen was the last room where he hadn't looked, so he would have headed that way next anyway. She thought that he had probably known from the start that she was there, but he wanted her to suffer longer.

McKenzie kicked the kitchen door open with his boot. Buddy flew at him, and as he lifted the rock to smash it down on the dog's head, Sarah shot him between the eyes. One small bullet took out the monster. His eyes widened, and it looked as if he was trying to blink before he fell on his back, dead. Or at least, that's what she hoped.

Buddy attacked the fallen man by grabbing the leg of his pants, shaking him around, and growling. Sarah, shaking, tried to take some deep breaths to calm herself down. It didn't work that well, but she felt there was no point in falling apart when the danger was over. She leaned over Buddy and patted him on the head, which seemed to calm him. He stopped shaking McKenzie around by his pants leg, climbed over him, and disappeared out of the house.

Sarah kneeled next to Mr. McKenzie. His open eyes were staring straight ahead into nothingness. She put her hand on his chest. Definitely dead. Mary's ghost flashed into existence for a few moments, and Sarah thought it looked as if she was smiling. Sarah smiled back, and Mary disappeared. For a few moments, Sarah worried that she would see McKenzie's ghost, but that never happened. She imagined him being carried straight off to hell, and it was satisfying.

She climbed over his body and walked through the house. He had done a good job in destroying the house. Just about every window had been broken, and he had kicked the door from its frame.

She walked outside, not wanting to see Josh's body, but she couldn't stop herself from doing it. In death, he looked like a rag doll that had been shaken apart. His face was purple and blue.

She felt tears running down her cheeks, but it wasn't sadness, more relief that she was finally free from his toxic presence forever. She wouldn't allow him to haunt her; she was finally done with him forever.

Sarah sat down next to Josh's body to wait for the Johnsons. When Buddy came running from the trees, he curled up next to her.

Chapter 12: The Bodies

It would be an understatement to say that the Johnsons' response to the two dead bodies was dramatic.

The Johnsons came driving up to Sarah's house so fast that they almost crashed their car into the tree under which Josh's body was lying. Mr. Johnson stumbled out of the car with a shotgun in his hands. Mildly amused, Sarah wondered if he always drove around with a shotgun in his car.

Mrs. Johnson jumped out the other side and ran straight to Sarah's side. They clearly weren't worried about any potential assailants that might still be around.

"Honey! Your leg! Let me look at it. I used to be a nurse."

Mrs. Johnson sat down next to Sarah and started unwrapping her leg. Mr. Johnson came and stood next to Josh with his shotgun pointed at the corpse.

"Is he dead? Where is the other one? Did he get away?"

Sarah nodded.

"He's dead. The other one is in the kitchen. He's also dead."

Mr. Johnson walked into the house, pointing the shotgun, just in case.

"Gawd! They did a number on your house."

Mr. Johnson disappeared inside. Mrs. Johnson patted her leg.

"At least you've stopped bleeding. I've got a first aid kit in the car. When my husband gives the all-clear, we can go into the house, and I'll patch you up."

Mr. Johnson shouted from the house.

"This one is definitely dead too! My Gawd, Amelia, you won't believe who it is. Explains why the grocery store is closed."

Mrs. Johnson walked into the house, and Sarah heard her shriek.

"McKenzie! The old fool. I always knew something wasn't right with him. He always looked at me funny, in a creepy way."

The Johnsons came walking out of the house. Mr. Johnson sighed and looked out over the yard.

"Well, it's a right mess we've got ourselves here. Why was McKenzie here? Why would he try to kill you? I never liked the man much, but it's a strange situation that we've got ourselves here."

Amelia Johnson frowned at her husband.

"We can hear the story while we patch up her leg. It's still bleeding slightly. Help me get her in the house."

The Johnsons helped her get into the house between the two of them. Mrs. Johnson fixed up her leg fast; as she had suspected, the bullet had gone right through, and there was no serious damage. Sarah told her story while they worked on her leg, flinching occasionally.

Amelia Johnson cried when she told her how Mr. Thompson and his daughter had met their deaths at the hands of Gerald McKenzie.

"That poor old man, and the girl, killed so many years ago. How awful is it that your child disappears, and you never know for sure what happened to them? Gerald McKenzie deserved what he got in the end. Hopefully, the old fool went straight to hell."

Mr. Johnson stood with his arms folded across his chest.

"Now, the question is, how do we deal with the bodies?"

Mrs. Johnson got up.

"I'm going to make us some coffee in the kitchen. Do you take sugar, my dear?"

Sarah nodded. She was grateful that the Johnsons were still here. Now that her leg had been disinfected and bandaged, she was starting to feel the pain. Every time she tried to move, a sharp pain shot up in her leg.

Mrs. Johnson returned with the coffees.

"We have to get the police. They will take the bodies away."

Sarah nodded, but Mr. Johnson frowned.

"Amelia, I don't know if that's the best idea. Josh has been saying awful things about Sarah to the media. He made her appear quite unbalanced. It'll be suspicious if he now turns up dead. And McKenzie... He's always been suspected of certain things. I've heard people call him a pervert. But the police will turn this place upside down if they find a scene like this. I don't think any of us want that. Sarah has experienced enough stress as it is."

Mrs. Johnson offered Sarah a cup.

"So what exactly are you saying? I'm starting to feel a bit uncomfortable."

Mr. Johnson stood up and started pacing the living room floor. He took care to step over the large pieces of glass.

"We bury them here, out in the woods. I know of a place where no one will ever find them. The police won't even look there; the woods, after all, have a reputation for being haunted."

Mrs. Johnson looked at her husband and shivered.

"Normally I wouldn't agree with something like this, but it's going to be kind of hard to explain what happened here. People will wonder what happened to McKenzie, but in the end, no one will care, or at least not for long. I heard someone say the other day at the ladies' tea that he used to beat his wife until she finally ran away. Despicable man."

Mr. Johnson smiled.

"It's settled then. I'll take the younger one first. Old McKenzie is going to be a heavy job and a half."

Sarah watched as he walked outside and prodded Josh's corpse with his shoe. He bent down and lifted the body over his shoulder. Sarah and Mrs. Johnson watched as he disappeared into the woods.

They talked while having coffee and biscuits. It seemed so surreal, considering what was happening around them. Mrs. Johnson told her that even though it would be difficult, she should try to put what happened behind her and get on with her life.

Sarah nodded, but at the same time, she could help but think how difficult it was going to be.

Mr. Johnson returned after about an hour. He looked tired and dirty.

"Phew, I managed to do it, but the soil was harder than I expected. Amelia, come and give me a hand to lift the old guy onto my back. He's as heavy as a sack of potatoes."

The Johnsons struggled with McKenzie's body, but they eventually managed to lift him. Mr. Johnson looked unsteady as he walked away with the corpse, but he soon managed to steady himself. He groaned.

"Ugh, the old fellow is heavy."

This time, Mr. Johnson stayed away much longer. Mrs. Johnson was starting to fret, because it was getting dark, and there wasn't a sign of him yet.

Then, when it was almost dark, they saw him walking from the woods.

Mrs. Johnson rushed out to meet her husband and hugged him. They came walking into the house together.

"Why did you take so long, my dear?"

Mr. Johnson sat down while his wife offered him a warm cup of coffee. He was panting.

"I had to get rid of the car, my dear. I think it belonged to the younger man; old McKenzie probably walked up through the woods. I think he doesn't live too far from them. He knew the woods like the back of his hand. I drove the car to the other side of the woods and left it there, in the abandoned part. I wiped it for my prints; hopefully I was thorough. That's why I took so long, I had to walk all the way back. But it's done now. We've handled it the best way we could. Let's hope we're forever done with these unpleasant people."

Mrs. Johnson kissed her husband, and Sarah hugged him.

"Come my dear, you'll have to stay with us tonight. We'll help you fix your house in the morning. Luckily we always keep extra glass and wood, so we'll be able to fix everything. My husband is a brilliant handyman; he'll get this place looking as good as new."

Sarah was grateful as they helped her get in the car, and coaxed Buddy to get in with them. That night she had the best night's sleep she'd had in a long time.

Chapter 13: Ending

By the end of the next day, her house looked better than it had before. She couldn't believe the speed and efficiency with which Mr. Johnson worked. He whistled while he worked, and occasionally he sang. His wife came with him to look after Sarah and to keep her company.

Amelia Johnson baked rusks and cookies while talking non-stop. It turned out she was an excellent baker. She also cooked soup and a stew, which she put in Sarah's freezer.

"My dear, you need some meat on your bones, and you shouldn't be skipping any meals. It's always useful to have quick and easy food available that you can quickly warm up. And it's useful to have some snacks around when you're feeling peckish but you don't really have the time to prepare anything."

When Mr. Johnson was done, and the Johnsons indicated that they wanted to go home, Sarah thanked them profusely and promised that she would visit regularly. Buddy barked at them, and they gave him farewell pets on the head.

She went to bed relieved, but she still locked up the entire house. Sarah hadn't been asleep for long when she started to dream. She hadn't seen any of the ghosts for a while, so she wasn't sure if they were still around, or if they had moved on. She was walking through the woods, on her way to the lake, when Mary appeared next to her. Mary looked clearer than she had ever seen her. The ghost was smiling, but she pointed at the lake. She stayed by Sarah's side during the walk, and Sarah realized that she clearly still needed her to do something.

"Do you need me to get your bones? Do you want me to bury you?"

The ghost nodded, smiled, and disappeared. Sarah continued sleeping, as it was such a peaceful dream. She only woke up when the sun was shining into her eyes the next morning.

She ate some of Mrs. Johnson's rusks for breakfast and gave Buddy breakfast outside while she sat watching him. She had another rusk, and then she was ready to do what needed to be done.

Sarah went to get the spade and some plastic bags. She was determined to put Mary to rest at last. Buddy followed her to the lake, but he started to whine when they got close to the boat. She reached down and patted him on the head.

"Don't worry about it, big guy. We just need to do this one last thing."

Today, the weather was warm and sunny, and she felt relaxed. It was a friendly day, as if nothing could go wrong. She instinctively felt that they had moved past the worst of the situation in the woods and town. They had defeated the evil, but there was still the last little bit that had to be done so that the woods could return to their natural state.

The lake was clear today, and the murkiness appeared to be gone. She didn't know if it was a natural phenomenon, but it felt to her as if a great evil had been lifted from the woods.

Sarah steered the boat out to the center of the lake where she dove into the depths once more. This time she could clearly see the skull gleaming below her. There were some bones scattered around it, and she resolved to take as many with her as she could.

She unfolded the plastic bag she had brought with her, and this time she managed to lift the skull into it. She took the other bones and swam back to the surface without any issues this time.

Buddy seemed relieved to see her, and he barked happily when she climbed back into the boat. Curious, he sniffed at the little bag of bones in her hand. This couldn't be all of Mary, but she hoped it was enough to put the girl at peace. She supposed some of the bones may have washed away, or old crazy McKenzie could have left some of them somewhere else.

Sarah took the bones and the spade and walked back to her house. The question was what to do with Mary. She felt like keeping Mary close to her. She smiled when she thought how strange she would have found this before. The woods must have changed her.

Mary appeared next to her. The girl was smiling.

"Mary, would you like to be close to me? Can I put you in the garden, close to my house?"

The girl smiled and nodded.

Sarah thought that it must be the strangest funeral ever, as the girl watched while she dug her grave. She placed the skull and bones inside. Afterwards, she put a wooden cross in the soil she had packed over the grave. She also planned to plant flowers over it.

When Sarah looked up from her work, she saw a bright light next to the tree in her driveway, with Mary standing next to it. Mary smiled and waved at her before stepping into the light and disappearing. Sarah waved back and wiped away a few tears.

As Sarah walked into her house, she suddenly had a strange idea. Maybe her next book would be a ghost story, and not a romance novel, as she was used to writing. She didn't know how her fans would react, but she felt that she needed to do it. She would dedicate the book to Mary and her father.

Sarah closed the door behind her and started cooking supper. She lit a fire in the fireplace, and the house felt warm and cozy. While Sarah was washing the dishes, she could see Mary's grave through the kitchen window. It felt as if the girl would forever be part of her, even though she had never known her when she was alive. Sarah smiled and went to feed Buddy.